Hired Help for Rabbit

story by Judy Delton
pictures by Lisa McCue

Macmillan Publishing Company   New York
Collier Macmillan Publishers   London

For Shirley Gould, and Delphinium Rose,
who's gorgeous right down to the hair on her toes
— J.D.

For Ken, with love
— L.M.

Text copyright © 1988 by Judy Delton. Illustrations copyright © 1988 by Lisa McCue.
 Macmillan Publishing Company,
866 Third Avenue, New York, NY 10022. Collier Macmillan Canada, Inc.
Printed and bound in Japan

First American Edition   10 9 8 7 6 5 4 3 2 1

The text of this book is set in 14 point Quorum Book.
The illustrations are rendered in watercolor, acrylic, and colored pencil on bristol.
Library of Congress Cataloging-in-Publication Data
Delton, Judy. Hired help for rabbit. Summary: Overwhelmed with housework, Rabbit decides to get help
in cooking, cleaning, and gardening.
[1. Rabbits — Fiction. 2. Household employees — Fiction] I. McCue, Lisa, ill.   II. Title.
PZ7.D388Hi 1988   [E]   87-15254   ISBN 0-02-728470-0

Rabbit weeded the last row in his carrot patch.
He had worked in his garden since early morning.
He stretched. "That is enough work for today,"
he said, and went into his house.

He looked at the clock and frowned. "It is later than I thought!"

Just then the phone rang. It was Rabbit's friend Duck.

"Duck," said Rabbit, after they had talked awhile. "Do you know where I can get a cook? I am too tired to cook after I garden all day."

Duck thought awhile. "No," she said. "But I will keep my eyes open for one, Rabbit."

Rabbit thanked Duck and hung up. As he was thinking about what to make for his supper, there was a knock on the door.

"Why, come in, Squirrel," said Rabbit. "I am not good company tonight. I have been so busy in my garden that I have not had time to cook my dinner yet. You don't know of any cook looking for work, do you, Squirrel?"

"Why, I cook very well, you know, Rabbit. You remember how you loved my wilted cabbage."

"The job is yours, Squirrel. When can you start?"

"Right now!" said Squirrel. "I'll cook you a fine dinner while you have a rest."

"Thank you, Squirrel!" Rabbit put his feet up on his footstool and relaxed. He listened to soft music on his radio. And he listened to dinner sounds coming from the kitchen. How lucky he was to find a cook! Rabbit dozed off, and when he awoke he smelled something strange. Smoke hung in the air over his chair. His eyes began to burn.

"Dinner is ready!" called Squirrel brightly.

Rabbit sat down at the table. On his plate was something black.

"Carrots in orange sauce," said Squirrel proudly.

"Shouldn't carrots be orange in color?" asked Rabbit.

Squirrel frowned. Then a tear ran down his face. "You loved my carrots in orange sauce at my house, Rabbit."

"Never mind," said Rabbit. "I am not too hungry now, anyway."

Squirrel brought in some turnips. They were raw. Then he brought in the dessert. It stuck to Rabbit's teeth and tasted like toothpaste.

The next day Rabbit showed Squirrel how to cook carrots in orange sauce. Then he showed him how to cook turnips. He was in the kitchen all day long. There was no time to garden.

The next day Squirrel overcooked the beans. He undercooked the parsnips. And the stove was coated with food that had boiled over. When Rabbit went to the kitchen, Squirrel was at the table sobbing.

Rabbit put his arm around his shoulder. "Don't worry, Squirrel. Not everyone is a cook. You just sit down, and I will get our dinner."

Rabbit put on his apron and cooked cabbage for two. They sat down and ate together. Squirrel looked happy again and took two more helpings of cabbage. Rabbit went to the kitchen and made some more.

That evening Weasel came by.

"Weasel," said Rabbit, "do you know where I can get a gardener? I am so busy cooking for Squirrel and me that I have no time to work in my garden."

"Why, I garden!" said Weasel. "I could start tomorrow."

"Really?" said Rabbit. "The sooner the better. Now I can stay inside and relax and just cook our meals."

The next day Rabbit looked out his window. Weasel was whistling as she worked. But she had pulled up all of Rabbit's lettuce from the ground.

"I thought it was weeds," she said, when Rabbit pointed at it.

"No, Weasel, THESE are weeds," he said, pointing to them. Rabbit spent the day trying to replant his lettuce.

The next day Weasel overwatered the peas. She underwatered the onions. She picked green tomatoes instead of red ones. When Rabbit showed her her mistakes, she felt bad. She sat on the replanted lettuce and sobbed.

"Don't worry," said Rabbit kindly. "Let me help you."

Every day Rabbit helped her in the garden. Every day Rabbit cooked meals for three. And every day Rabbit was more tired than he had been before he had hired help.

One morning Rabbit got out of bed and noticed that the kitchen floor was full of crumbs. Dirty dishes stood in the sink. And gardening tools were everywhere.

"I believe I need a housecleaner." He sighed.

From his window he could see Hedgehog shaking his rugs.

"Hedgehog!" he called. "Would you be interested in cleaning for me?"

Hedgehog came over to Rabbit's door, still shaking his rug. "Do you mean you want to hire me?" he said.

"Why, yes," said Rabbit. "I have been so busy cooking and gardening that the house has become very messy."

"Well, I wouldn't mind extra work. I'm a very good housecleaner, if I say so myself."

"When can you start?" said Rabbit.

"Why, I'll start today," he replied.

Rabbit felt relieved. "Now," he said to himself, "I'll have plenty of hired help."

On the way to the garden
to pull a carrot, Rabbit went
through the kitchen. "Dear me!
You don't put flour in
strawberry jam!" he said to
Squirrel kindly. He measured
the sugar for Squirrel and
put the flour away and
went to the garden to
pull his carrots.

He got there just in time
to stop Weasel from picking
the green corn. "You must
wait until it is ripe,"
he said kindly.

Rabbit went into
the house for a short
nap. But when he
got there, the mattress
was not on his bed!
His blankets and sheets
were missing, too!

"They are airing,"
said Hedgehog.
"Bedding needs fresh
air, Rabbit."

Rabbit went to the living room to sit in his
favorite chair. But his favorite chair was gone.

"I called the repair shop," said Hedgehog.
"A spring was broken in your
chair, and they took
it away to be fixed.
You can sit on the
floor, Rabbit."

Rabbit stretched out on the floor. It made his bones ache. He dozed off for a moment, and when he woke up he heard thunder.

"Hedgehog!" he called. "My mattress and bedding are getting soaked!"

Hedgehog was drinking a cup of tea with Weasel in the kitchen. "I need a rest, Rabbit. I can't do everything at once!"

Rabbit ran out and dragged his wet mattress into the house. He brought in his wet blankets and sheets, too.

While his bedding was drying, Rabbit cooked dinner for four.

The next day, he helped Weasel in the garden.
Then he put the still-wet bedding out in the sun to
dry. And that evening he was even more
tired than he had been before
he had hired help.

At the end of the week, Squirrel came to Rabbit and said, "Rabbit, I am sorry to say this, but I am afraid I must leave. I don't want to hurt your feelings, but you are just too fussy about your meals."

"Dear me, that is bad news," said Rabbit. "I shall miss you, Squirrel. Let me help you pack your things."

When his suitcase was packed, Squirrel waved good-bye and set off for home with a tear in his eye.

"It's hard to lose a cook," said Rabbit, putting his kitchen back in order and scrubbing the last spill marks from his stove.

The next day Weasel came to Rabbit and said, "Rabbit, I hate to say this, but I'm afraid I am overworked here. Your garden is very large, and the doctor said I am not a young weasel anymore."

"Why, that is bad news," said Rabbit. "I shall miss you, Weasel. I will have to get used to having no gardener now."

Rabbit helped Weasel pack her suitcase. Then he waved as Weasel set off down the garden path to her own home.

"It is hard to lose a gardener," said Rabbit as he went into his garden and planted new lettuce. He picked only the red tomatoes and had them for his supper.

The next day Rabbit felt full of pep again, even though he was sleeping on the floor because his mattress was still damp.

As he was making breakfast for himself and Hedgehog, Hedgehog came into the kitchen and cleared his throat. "Rabbit," he said nervously, "I have something on the order of bad news. The extra job is more than I can handle. Quite frankly, Rabbit, you have let the place go. You could use two housecleaners, you know."

"Do you have to leave?" asked Rabbit. "Is that what you are saying?"

"I'm afraid so," admitted Hedgehog.

"I'll help you pack," said Rabbit kindly.

When Hedgehog left, Rabbit sighed. "It's not easy," he said, "losing all of one's hired help. I will just have to make the best of it."

That afternoon Rabbit put the dried mattress back on his bed. He put clean sheets and blankets on it. Then he went to the shop and got back his chair with the broken spring. He sat in it and put his feet up and rested. When he was hungry he cooked supper. For one.

After supper, the phone rang. It was Duck.

"Hello, Rabbit," she said. "I heard that you found yourself a cook and a gardener and a housecleaner. How have things worked out?"

"Things have worked out very well, Duck. Very well indeed."

"And are you less tired now, Rabbit?"

"Yes, Duck," replied Rabbit with his feet up on the footstool. "I can honestly say I am less tired today than I have been in a long, long while."

"Well, good, Rabbit. There is nothing like good hired help, is there?"

"No, Duck, there is nothing like it," he said, hanging up the phone.

"Except NO hired help!" Rabbit chuckled to himself. Then he washed one plate and went to bed.

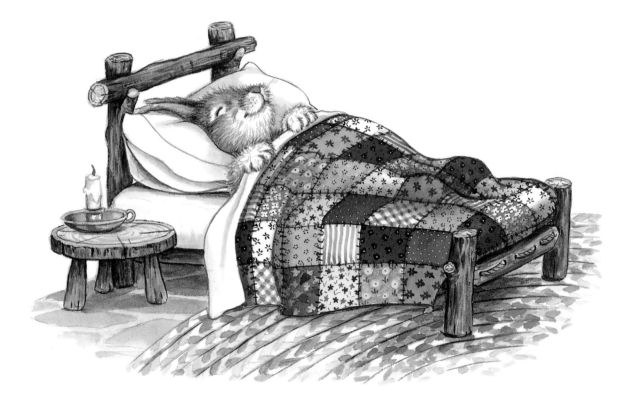